SHERLOCK HOLMES

and the Adventure of Black Peter

Based on the stories of
Sir Arthur Conan Doyle

Adapted by **Murray Shaw** and **M. J. Cosson**
Illustrated by **Sophie Rohrbach** and **JT Morrow**

GRAPHIC UNIVERSE™ · MINNEAPOLIS · NEW YORK

Grateful acknowledgment to Dame Jean Conan Doyle for permission to use the
Sherlock Holmes characters created by Sir Arthur Conan Doyle

Graphic Universe™
A division of Lerner Publishing Group, Inc.
241 First Avenue North
Minneapolis, MN 55401 U.S.A.

Website address: www.lernerbooks.com

Library of Congress Cataloging-in-Publication Data

Shaw, Murray.
    Sherlock Holmes and the adventure of Black Peter / based on the stories
of Sir Arthur Conan Doyle ; adapted by Murray Shaw and M. J. Cosson ;
illustrated by Sophie Rohrbach and JT Morrow.
       p.   cm. — (On the case with Holmes and Watson ; #11)
    Summary: Retold in graphic novel form, Sherlock Holmes investigates the
gruesome murder by harpoon of a very unpleasant former sea captain known
as Black Peter. Includes a section explaining Holmes's reasoning and the
clues he used to solve the mystery.
    ISBN: 978-0-7613-7092-5 (lib. bdg. : alk. paper)
    I. Graphic novels. (I. Graphic novels. 2. Doyle, Arthur Conan, Sir,
1859-1930. Adventure of Black Peter—Adaptations. 3. Mystery and detective
stories.) I. Cosson, M. J. II. Rohrbach, Sophie, ill III. Morrow, JT, ill. IV.
Doyle, Arthur Conan, Sir, 1859-1930. Adventure of Black Peter. V. Title.
PZ7.7.S46Shhm 2012   2011005115
741.5'973—dc22

Manufactured in the United States of America
1—BC—12/31/11

The Story of
SHERLOCK HOLMES
the Famous Detective

Sherlock Holmes and his helpful friend Dr. John Watson are fictional characters created by British writer Sir Arthur Conan Doyle. Doyle published his first novel about the pair, *A Study in Scarlet*, in 1887, and it became very successful. Doyle went on to write fifty-six short stories, as well as three more novels about Holmes's adventures—*The Sign of Four* (1890), *The Hound of the Baskervilles* (1902), and *The Valley of Fear* (1915).

Sherlock Holmes and Dr. Watson have become some of the most famous book characters of all time. Holmes spent most of his time solving mysteries, but he also had a wide array of hobbies, such as playing the violin, boxing, and sword fighting. Watson, a retired army doctor, met Holmes through a mutual friend when Holmes was looking for a roommate. Watson lived with Holmes for several years at 221B Baker Street before marrying and moving out. However, after his marriage, Watson continued to assist Holmes with his cases.

The original versions of the Sherlock Holmes stories are still printed, and many have been made into movies and television shows. Readers continue to be impressed by Holmes's detective methods of observation and scientific reason.

From the Desk of
John H. Watson, M.D.

My name is Dr. John H. Watson. For several years, I have been assisting my friend, Sherlock Holmes, in solving mysteries throughout the bustling city of London and beyond. Holmes is a peculiar man—always questioning and reasoning his way through various problems. But when I first met him in 1878, I was immediately intrigued by his oddities.

Holmes has always been more daring than I, and his logical deduction never ceases to amaze me. I have begun writing down all of the adventures I have with Holmes. This is one of those stories.

Sincerely,

Dr. Watson

THE FIRST WEEK IN JULY 1895 HAD BEEN A BUSY ONE FOR HOLMES AND ME. HOLMES HAD BEEN GONE QUITE OFTEN, SO I KNEW HE WAS HARD AT WORK ON A CASE.

I'M HERE TO SEE CAPTAIN BASIL.

CAPTAIN BASIL ISN'T HERE AT THE MOMENT.

HOLMES MIGHT BE USING THE NAME OF CAPTAIN BASIL TO INVESTIGATE A CASE, I THOUGHT, WHEN ANOTHER ROUGH-LOOKING CHARACTER SHOWED UP.

I'M HERE TO SEE CAPTAIN BASIL. I HEARD HE'S LOOKING FOR A CREW.

CAPTAIN BASIL ISN'T HERE. PLEASE CALL AGAIN.

THEN FRIDAY MORNING AFTER BREAKFAST . . .

GOOD HEAVENS! HAVE YOU BEEN CARRYING THAT THING ALL OVER LONDON?

CERTAINLY NOT, WATSON. I TOOK A CAB TO AND FROM ALLARDYCE'S BUTCHER SHOP. HAD YOU BEEN WITH ME, YOU WOULD HAVE SEEN ME STABBING ONE OF THEIR HANGING PIGS WITH THIS SPEAR.

PLEASE, BE SEATED. I'VE READ THE NEWSPAPER SUMMARY OF THE WOODMAN'S LEE CASE DOWN IN SUSSEX. I'D LIKE TO HEAR SCOTLAND YARD'S ACCOUNT.

THE FACTS ARE THESE, MR. HOLMES. PETER CAREY WAS BORN IN 1845. AS A YOUNG MAN, HE WENT TO SEA ON A BEAUTIFUL MERCHANT SHIP.

IN 1882, HE BECAME THE SUCCESSFUL CAPTAIN OF A SCOTTISH WHALING AND SEALING STEAMER, NAMED THE *SEA UNICORN*.

CAREY WAS A HARSH CAPTAIN. HE WAS CALLED BLACK PETER BECAUSE OF HIS THICK, BLACK BEARD AND HIS VIOLENT TEMPER.

THE CABIN HAS A WINDOW THAT FACES THE ROAD. TWO NIGHTS BEFORE THE CRIME, A STONECUTTER NAMED SLATER PASSED THE CABIN ON HIS WAY HOME FROM THE LOCAL TAVERN.

SLATER SWEARS THAT AS HE PASSED, HE SAW THE OUTLINE OF A MAN IN THE LIGHTED WINDOW. HE INSISTS THAT IT WASN'T CAREY HE SAW. CAREY HAD A FULL, BUSHY BEARD. SLATER CLAIMS THIS MAN HAD A SHORT BEARD THAT STUCK OUT FROM HIS CHIN.

THIS MAY NOT HAVE ANY CONNECTION WITH THE MURDER. THE CABIN IS A DISTANCE FROM THE ROAD. SLATER'S TAVERN FRIENDS SAY HE WAS DRINKING HEAVILY THAT NIGHT.

LATE ON THE NIGHT OF HIS TERRIBLE DEATH, CAREY STAGGERED TO HIS CABIN. HE HAD BEEN ANGRY ALL DAY.

SOMETIME IN THE MIDDLE OF THAT NIGHT, HIS DAUGHTER WAS AWAKENED BY A PIERCING CRY. BUT SHE WAS USED TO HER FATHER'S RAGES. SHE WENT BACK TO SLEEP AND THOUGHT NO MORE ABOUT IT.

AAAAAAGGGGHHHHHH!

THE NEXT MORNING, ONE OF THE MAIDS NOTICED THE CABIN DOOR WAS OPEN. SHE APPROACHED AND PEERED IN. THEN SHE WENT OFF SCREAMING, AND I WAS SENT FOR.

AAAHHHH!

GENTLEMEN, I HAVE STEADY NERVES, BUT NO SOLDIER'S TRAINING COULD HAVE PREPARED ME FOR THE SIGHT IN THAT CABIN.

Holmes examined the notebook. Handwritten on the first page were the initials J.H.N. and the year 1883. On the pages that followed were headings, such as C.P.R., Argentina, and Australia. Beneath each heading was a list of numbers or company names.

19

That afternoon, after arriving at the train station in the village of Woodman's Lee, we took a carriage to Carey's house. His wife and daughter greeted us. They gave us permission to examine the cabin but refused to come with us. Taking the well-worn path, we headed through the woods to the one-room cabin.

It was a gloomy task to crouch among the bushes through the sunset and oncoming night. Yet there was a kind of strange thrill to it all—such as a hunter feels. What murderous beast would we meet in the darkness? What raging fight would it take to capture the creature?

A fine drizzle began to fall, and over the sound of the rain on the leaves, we could hear the church bells chime—first midnight, then one o'clock, and then two. Each time a villager passed on the road, we would stiffen and wait for approaching steps.

AFTER HE LEFT, WE HEARD THAT A FIERCE STORM CAME UP IN THE NORTH SEA ALONG HIS ROUTE. WE NEVER HEARD FROM HIM AGAIN.

WE FINALLY HAD TO ACCEPT THAT HE AND HIS SMALL TIN BOX OF CERTIFICATES WERE AT THE BOTTOM OF THE SEA.

THEN A FEW YEARS AGO, A FAMILY FRIEND DISCOVERED THAT A NUMBER OF MY FATHER'S CERTIFICATES HAD SHOWN UP FOR SALE IN LONDON. THEY HAD BEEN PUT ON THE MARKET BY A CAPTAIN PETER CAREY.

I FIGURED THE CAPTAIN MUST KNOW SOMETHING ABOUT MY FATHER IF HE HAD THE CERTIFICATES. SO I TRACKED HIM HERE.

BY THE TIME I ARRIVED AT THE VILLAGE, THE CAPTAIN WAS DEAD. BUT THE NEWSPAPER REPORT SAID THAT THE LOGBOOKS FROM HIS VOYAGES WERE IN THE CABIN.

SO I CAME HERE LAST NIGHT AND TRIED TO GET IN. THE WINDOWS AND DOOR WERE LOCKED. I RETURNED TO THE VILLAGE TO GET A STEEL PRY AND CAME BACK TO TRY AGAIN.

BUT IT'S JUST MY LUCK—THE LOGBOOK PAGES FROM THE SUMMER OF 1883 ARE MISSING, THE CERTIFICATES ARE NOWHERE IN SIGHT, AND NOW YOU THINK I'M A MURDERER.

BUT I'M *NOT*, I TELL YOU.

IF THIS IS THE FIRST TIME YOU'VE BEEN IN THIS ROOM, HOW DID YOUR NOTEBOOK GET HERE?

29

I lay back in my seat and tried to sleep. I knew better than to question Holmes further. He wasn't going to tell me about his investigative methods until they had proven successful. So now I had one more mystery to ponder—why was Holmes playing the part of Captain Basil?

Early the next morning, two telegrams arrived for Holmes. He opened them eagerly and then broke into a quiet chuckle of satisfaction. He told me briefly of their contents. One was a list of names from a whaling company in Scotland. The other was a brief message from the shipping agent, listing the sailors who would visit Captain Basil the next morning.

34

A FEW OF US PULLED THE SINGLE SAILOR OUT OF THE BOAT AND ONTO THE DECK. HE WAS WET TO THE BONE, BUT HE WOULDN'T LET GO OF THIS SMALL BOX HE CARRIED.

TAKE HIM TO MY QUARTERS, AND SEE THAT HE DOESN'T LEAVE. I'LL BE DOWN DIRECTLY.

SOMETIME AROUND MIDNIGHT, AFTER THE STORM HAD BROKEN SOME, I SAW CAREY AND THE STRANGER NEAR THE SIDE RAIL.

WELL, HOPKINS, YOU'LL HAVE TO RETRIEVE THAT LITTLE TIN BOX AND RETURN IT TO POOR NELIGAN WITH AN APOLOGY. NOW HE CAN FINALLY CLEAR HIS FATHER'S NAME.

MR. HOLMES, YOU ARE THE MASTER, AND I AM YOUR HUMBLE PUPIL. I DON'T KNOW HOW YOU DID IT, BUT I'M GRATEFUL.

TAKING HIS PRISONER TO A WAITING CAB, HOPKINS DEPARTED FOR SCOTLAND YARD.

The Adventure of Black Peter: How Did Holmes Solve It?

How did Holmes know that Neligan did not kill Carey?

After reading about Carey's unusual murder, Holmes reasoned that the killer had to be powerful and skilled with a harpoon. To prove it, Holmes practiced on a dead pig. No matter how hard he tried, he couldn't drive a spear through the pig with one blow. When he met Neligan, he concluded that Neligan was not strong enough or experienced enough to have killed Carey.

How did Holmes know that the tobacco pouch belonged to Carey's killer?

The sealskin pouch had the initials P.C. printed on it. But Holmes did not assume that it belonged to the captain. Since a pipe was not found in the cabin, Holmes suspected that the pouch could belong to the unidentified killer.

How did Holmes figure out that Cairns was Carey's killer?

Carey was only a captain for a short time. Holmes suspected that there was an unusual reason for Carey's early retirement. Therefore, he was curious about Carey's life on the ship just before his retirement. Since harpooners work on whaling and sealing ships, Holmes figured that the killer was probably a harpooner on the *Sea Unicorn*. So he wired the company in Scotland for the ship's 1883 crew roster. This list of names came in one of the telegrams. Holmes looked down the list and found a harpooner with the initials P.C.—Patrick Cairns.

Why did Holmes suspect that the tin box was an important clue in the crime?

Neligan mentioned that his father's certificates had been kept in a small tin box. And it was known that Carey had had the certificates. For that reason, Holmes suspected the object removed from the logbook shelf was the tin box.

How did Holmes know that he could lure Cairns to his apartment with the promise of a job?

Holmes reasoned that the harpooner who killed Carey would want to leave England as quickly as possible. So under the name of Captain Basil, Holmes offered high wages and a long sea voyage to draw the murderer out. The shipping company sent Holmes the likely candidates. Once Holmes met Cairns, he knew he had the right man.

Further Reading and Websites

Cook, Peter. *You Wouldn't Want to Sail on a 19th Century Whaling Ship!: Grisly Tasks You'd Rather Not Do.* New York: Children's Press, 2004.

Cosson, M. J. *Yankee Whalers.* New York: Rourke Publishing, 2007.

Currie, Stephen. *Thar She Blows: American Whaling in the Nineteenth Century.* Minneapolis: Twenty-First Century Books, 2001.

Kassirer, Sue. *Thar She Blows: Whaling in the 1860s.* Norwalk, CT: Soundprints, 1997.

Kittredge, Frances. *Neeluk: An Eskimo Boy in the Days of the Whaling Ships.* Portland, OR: Graphic Arts Center Publishing Company, 2003.

Melville, Herman. *Moby Dick: Or, the Whale.* New York: Simon & Schuster, 2001.

Melville, Herman. *Moby Dick: The Graphic Novel.* New York: Barron's Educational, 2007.

Sandler, Martin. *Trapped in Ice!: An Amazing True Whaling Adventure.* New York: Scholastic Press, 2006.

Sherlock Holmes Museum
http://www.sherlock-holmes.co.uk

Sir Arthur Conan Doyle Society
http://www.ash-tree.bc.ca/acdsocy.html

221 Baker Street
http://221bakerstreet.org

About the Author

Sir Arthur Conan Doyle was born on May 22, 1859. He became a doctor in 1882. When this career did not prove successful, Doyle started writing stories. In addition to the popular Sherlock Holmes short stories and novels, Doyle also wrote historical novels, romances, and plays.

About the Adapters

Murray Shaw's lifelong passion for Sherlock Holmes began when he was a child. He was the author of the Match Wits with Sherlock Holmes series published in the 1990s. For decades, he was a popular speaker in public schools and libraries on the adventures of Holmes and Watson.

M. J. Cosson is the author of more than fifty books, both fiction and nonfiction, for children and young adults. She has long been a fan of mysteries and especially of the great detective, Sherlock Holmes. In fact, she has participated in the production of several Sherlock Holmes plays. A native of Iowa, Cosson lives in the Texas Hill Country with her husband, dogs, and cat.

About the Illustrators

French artist Sophie Rohrbach began her career after graduating in display design at the Chambre des Commerce. She went on to design displays in many top department stores including Galerias Lafayette. She also studied illustration at Emile Cohl school in Lyon, France, where she now lives with her daughter. Rohrbach has illustrated many children's books. She is passionate about the colors and patterns that she uses in her illustrations.

JT Morrow has worked as a freelance illustrator for over twenty years and has won several awards. He specializes in doing parodies and imitations of the Old and Modern Masters—everyone from da Vinci to Picasso. JT also exhibits his paintings at galleries near his home. He lives just south of San Francisco with his wife and daughter.